# The Wonderful World of My Wacky Grandpa

## ADVENTURES OF ZIGGY AND JACQUES

Published by:
BookBaby, 7905 North Route 130
Pennsauken, NJ 08110
2021

Created By:
Betty Bartha, Educator
Karen Katchen, Psychologist
Illustrated By: Karen Katchen

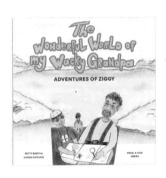

# The Wonderful World of My Wacky Grandpa

## ADVENTURES OF ZIGGY AND JACQUES

Inspired by our grandchildren

Lily, Benjy, Asa, Ruby Pauline,
Joshua, Ruby Max, Saul and Jack

It is Grandpa sitting on his favorite bench
With me, Jacques the parrot, all a-flutter.
What can I say about incredible Grandpa?
He always has wise words to utter.

Grandpa's not bumfuzzled or confused.
He creates mysteries to unwrap.
"A-Hah! I see something of interest.
Could that be a treasure map?"

I may be talkative and colorful,
Looking very proud and bold,
But Grandpa has the sunshine smile,
And a heart of solid gold.

Red suspenders tightly fastened,
Cap sitting atop his curly hair.
I am comfy on Grandpa's shoulder,
There is so much ahead to share.

"Jacques, time for us to get along,"
Grandpa proclaims with a shout.
"Ziggy is waiting excitedly
To see what his adventure is about."

Hear the clicking of the peddles,
Grandpa and Jacques are on their way.
Approaching Ziggy in is own front yard –
"It's them," he cheers, "Hip, Hip, Hooray!"

"Ziggy, we will be detectives
With a magnifying glass and binoculars too.
Hop onto this bicycle express,
Many surprises are waiting for you!"

"There are wonders all around us
That you will gaze upon with delight.
Our time together is so special,
Whether morning, noon or night."

Get ready for some riddles
That are challenging and fun.
You'll be astonished and amazed
With your answers to each one!

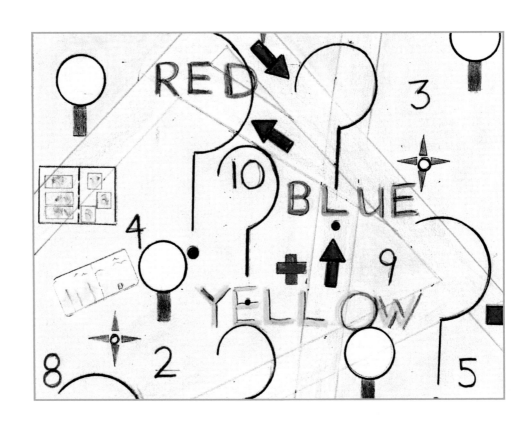

# Riddle 1 – Oh Such Fun!

No need to be quiet
Beautiful petals you can keep
Colorful plants come here often
To get a lot of sleep.

What am I?

# Did you guess a Flowerbed?

Grandpa says, "Hold on tight.
Let's piggyback down the block.
Close your eyes Ziggy,
The next clue is here to unlock."

# Riddle 2—Just For You.

This is always running,
Never does it walk.
Its head has no eyes to cry
And a mouth that cannot talk.

What am I?

# Did you guess a River?

From the river to the corner
While waiting for a bus.
As we board, Grandpa says,
"Such a thrill ahead for us."

When we get off downtown
And step inside the store,
Ziggy exclaims,"I don't know where to cast my eyes
There are instruments here galore!

Clap your hands and jump for joy,
More mysteries still to come.
Lots of giggles are ahead,
We've only just begun.

# Riddle 3 – What Can It Be?

I have many keys but I have no locks.
People call me "grand" or "upright."
When you sit upon a stool,
Your fingers move on black and white.

What am I?

# Did you guess a Piano?

"Ziggy, we will get our thinking beanies on,
And our backpacks for a hike.
There is nothing on our journey
That you truly will not like.

# Riddle 4 – What's The Score?

I have many plates,
But no food on them to eat.
There are bats, but not in caves
Walking and running with your feet.

What am I?

# Did you guess a Baseball Diamond?

"Ziggy, let's put our yellow helmets on,
Then carefully balance on our feet.
The scooters will take us to our next surprise
While we are gliding down the street."

# Riddle 5 – Something To Drive?

Although I'm not a bird,
My wings do help me fly.
I also have a nose and tail.
You can see me in the sky.

What am I?

# Did You Guess An Airplane?

Honk! Honk! Varoom! Varoom!
I recognize that sound coming from afar.
Wow! It's Grandma driving towards us,
In her red polka-a-dotted car!

We're about to climb in, when Grandpa says,
"Here's the picture you need to know.
Ziggy, the final clue is on the map,
That is where we have to go."

Grandma and Grandpa lead me in
To their library down the hall.
"Search for the treasure album, Ziggy,
You will find it on the wall!"

Ziggy exclaims, "Here it is!"
As he turns the pages of his memory book.
"I will remember this forever,
With each and every look."

Jacques says, "Gather round riddle-solvers.
It's a snug-a-hug for everyone.
These adventures might be over,
But our curiosity is never done!"

# The Wonderful World of
# My Wacky Grandpa

## ADVENTURES OF ZIGGY AND JACQUES

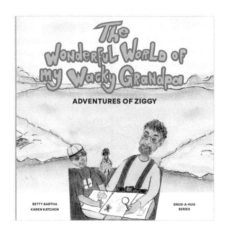